A NOTE TO PARENTS

When your children are ready to "step into reading," giving them the right books—and lots of them—is as crucial as giving them the right food to eat. **Step into Reading Books** present exciting stories and information reinforced with lively, colorful illustrations that make learning to read fun, satisfying, and worthwhile. They are priced so that acquiring an entire library of them is affordable. And they are beginning readers with an important difference—they're written on four levels.

Step 1 Books, with their very large type and extremely simple vocabulary, have been created for the very youngest readers. **Step 2 Books** are both longer and slightly more difficult. **Step 3 Books,** written to mid-second-grade reading levels, are for the child who has acquired even greater reading skills. **Step 4 Books** offer exciting nonfiction for the increasingly proficient reader.

Children develop at different ages. **Step into Reading Books,** with their four levels of reading, are designed to help children become good—and interested—readers *faster*. The grade levels assigned to the four steps—preschool through grade 1 for Step 1, grades 1 through 3 for Step 2, grades 2 and 3 for Step 3, and grades 2 through 4 for Step 4—are intended only as guides. Some children move through all four steps very rapidly; others climb the steps over a period of several years. These books will help your child "step into reading" in style!

For Ole Risom

Library of Congress Cataloging-in-Publication Data:
Buller, Jon. No tooth, no quarter! : by Jon Buller and Susan Schade.   p.   cm.–(Step into reading. A Step 3 book)
SUMMARY: Fearing punishment from Queen Denteena for not finding any good teeth, an unlucky tooth fairy takes a boy down into the underground kingdom of the tooth fairies so he can explain that his tooth fell out but he mislaid it.   ISBN: 0-394-84956-6 (pbk.); 0-394-94956-0 (lib. bdg.)   [1. Tooth Fairy–Fiction. 2. Teeth–Fiction]
I. Schade, Susan. II. Title. III. Series   PZ7.B9135No   1990   [E]–dc19   89-30250

Manufactured in the United States of America   6 7 8 9 0

STEP INTO READING is a trademark of Random House, Inc.

Step into Reading

No Tooth, No Quarter!

By Jon Buller and Susan Schade

A Step 3 Book

Random House New York

Two tooth fairies were sitting on a branch. The small one was reading her report card.

Dog Tooth . . . . .F

Fake Vampire Teeth . . . . .F

Cracked Tooth With Fillings . . . . .F

"All F's again!" she wailed.

Her friend patted her on the back. "Don't worry," she said to the little tooth fairy. "You'll find a good tooth soon."

"I'd better! If I don't find a perfect tooth tonight, Queen Denteena will take away my wings. I'll be grounded! And I won't be able to go to the Decay Prevention Ball!"

So the little tooth fairy flew off to look for
a perfect tooth.

Soon she came to a schoolyard, where some kids were playing dodge ball.

"Think fast, Walter!" A girl threw the ball at the boy in the middle.

Walter jumped out of the way. "Missed!" he shouted. But as he landed he tripped and fell over a rock.

"Oh dear," gasped the tooth fairy. "I hope he didn't hurt himself."

"Look!" Walter picked himself up,
grinning. "My tooth fell out!" He held it up
and then put it in his pocket. "This goes
under my pillow tonight!"

"At last!" whispered the tooth fairy.
"This is my lucky day! I'll follow him home
after school."

And that's just what she did.

She waited outside his house until dark.

She watched the lights go out one by one.

Soon there was nothing but a soft glow coming from one window.

It was Walter's window.

The tooth fairy flew in.

She squeezed under Walter's pillow and felt around.

All she found was a letter. It said:

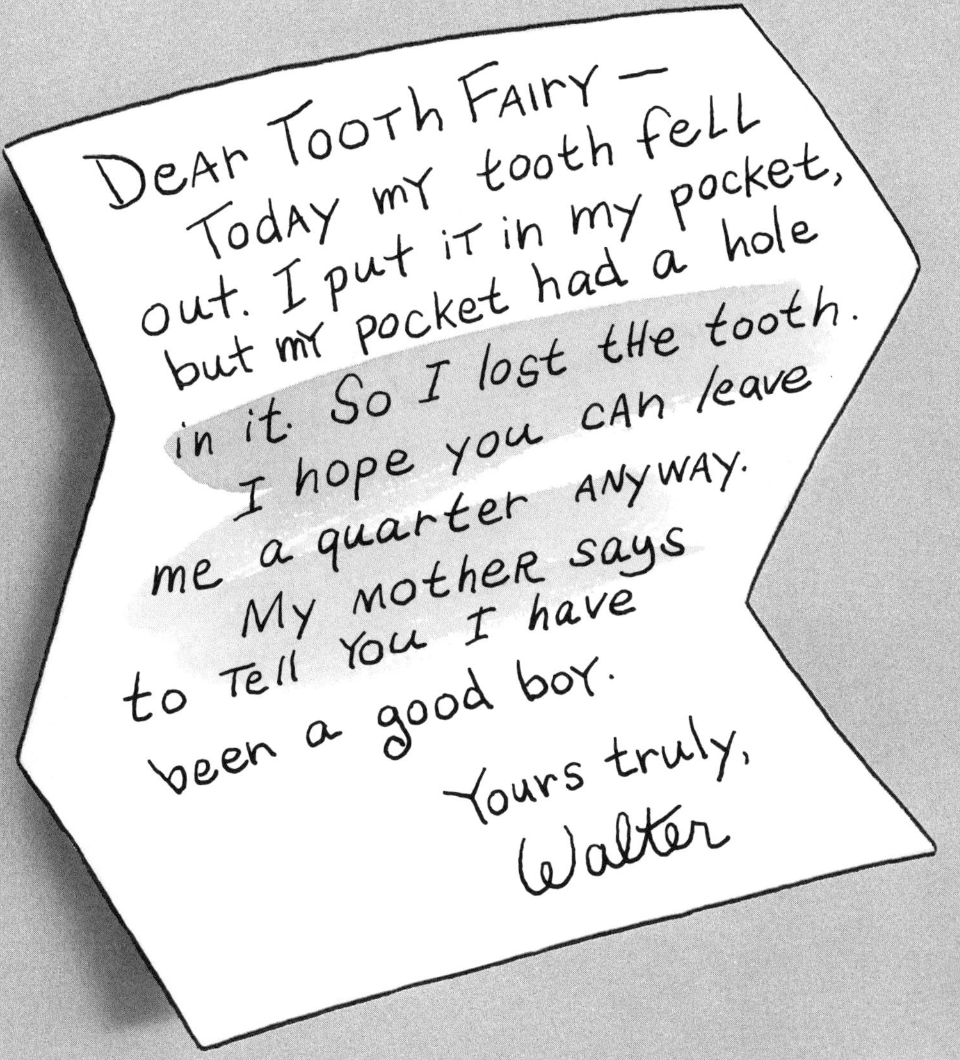

Dear Tooth Fairy —
Today my tooth fell out. I put it in my pocket, but my pocket had a hole in it. So I lost the tooth. I hope you can leave me a quarter anyway. My mother says to tell you I have been a good boy.

Yours truly,
Walter

"NO TOOTH!" the tooth fairy cried.
"Oh, no!"

She flew up to Walter's chin.

"Maybe he has another one that's ready to go." She grabbed one of Walter's teeth and gave a big yank.

"HEY!" yelled Walter. He sat up in bed. "WOW! It's the tooth fairy! Did you get my letter?"

She nodded. "But I can't leave you a quarter, Walter. Our first rule is NO TOOTH, NO QUARTER, and Queen Denteena is very strict."

Then the little fairy started to cry. "This was my last chance to find a perfect tooth! Now Queen Denteena will take away my wings!"

"But that's not fair!" Walter said. "It isn't *your* fault I lost my tooth. Why don't you explain it to her?"

"You don't know Queen Denteena," said the tooth fairy. "I'm really scared of her."

"Well, I'm not!" said Walter. "I'll tell her."

"All right," said the tooth fairy. "I'll try anything." And she waved her wand at Walter.

WHOOSH! He was as small as she was.
"YOW!" he cried.

"Come on," said the tooth fairy. She grabbed Walter's hand, and they flew right out the open window!

They zipped down to a hole at the bottom of a tree.

They flew through a long, winding tunnel under the ground.

At last they came out in Tooth Fairy Land.

"It's an underground world!" Walter gasped.

"Isn't it beautiful?" asked the tooth fairy.

"We grow all of our own food here, and
we make all of our own clothes.

"The only thing we need from you is a
little help with our houses."

Walter looked at the gleaming white houses. They were made of bricks. Little fairies were everywhere, polishing them with brushes.

"The bricks are teeth!" cried Walter. "I always wondered what you did with them."

"Well, here we are," said the tooth fairy. "This is where Queen Denteena lives—the Ivory Palace."

They went through the gates. Inside the palace was a long hallway.

At last they came to the throne room. And there was Queen Denteena!

"What's this?" she shrieked. "A BOY?"

"This is Walter," said Walter's tooth fairy. "He lost his tooth."

"We don't want HIM," said Queen Denteena. "Just the tooth."

"She means I can't *find* my tooth that fell out," explained Walter. "It disappeared. But I really did lose one. You can see the hole." Walter opened wide and pointed to show the queen.

"IDIOT!" yelled Queen Denteena. "I suppose you put the tooth in your pocket?"

"Well, yes," said Walter.

"And your pocket had a hole in it?"

"Well, yes," said Walter.

"And now you want a quarter anyway? IDIOT! Do you think you can get something for nothing? Out of my sight!"

"All right," he said, "but I just wanted to say it wasn't the tooth fairy's fault." And he turned to go.

"WAIT!" shouted Queen Denteena. "What beautiful purple pajamas! Those are just what I need for the Decay Prevention Ball. I'll give you twenty-five cents for the purple pajamas. We'll forget the tooth."

"I'm not that stupid," said Walter.
"These pajamas probably cost ten dollars.
Besides, I would catch cold."

"STOP!" she cried. "I want those
pajamas. Seize him!"

Walter ran.

The little tooth fairy ran too.

The tooth soldiers chased after them.

In the distance Walter could hear Queen Denteena screaming, "Get those purple pajamas!"

Then the tooth fairy caught Walter's
hand, and up they flew.

They went back through the tunnel,
back out the hole in the tree,

and back in the open window.

Walter was big again! He was in his own room and he was still wearing his pajamas.

The tooth fairy looked glum. A tear rolled down her cheek. "Baw-haw!" she cried.

"Hey," said Walter, "what's the matter? We made it. You saved me."

"But what about me?" cried the tooth fairy. "Now I can't go home."

"I have an idea. You can move in with us," said Walter. "My parents are pretty nice."

"Baw!" cried the tooth fairy.

"All right, all right," said Walter. "Let me think."

"I know!" he said. "Where are my scissors?" He opened his desk. "Here they are.

"I'm much bigger now," Walter said. "Right?"

The tooth fairy agreed.

"And my pajamas are bigger too, right?"

The tooth fairy nodded.

"Then watch this!" And he snipped the inside of his pocket right off.

He handed it to the tooth fairy. It was as big as she was.

"Do you think that will make Queen Denteena happy?"

The tooth fairy grinned. "It's perfect, Walter. Thank you so much."

Walter climbed back into bed. "Will you wake me up when you come for my next tooth?" he asked sleepily.

"Sure," said the tooth fairy. "Only try not to lose it before I get here."

"It's a deal." Then Walter fell fast asleep. He didn't see the tooth fairy tap her wand under his pillow.

But the next morning he found a quarter there.

As for the little tooth fairy, she had a
wonderful time at the Decay Prevention Ball.
And Queen Denteena gave her all A's on
her next report card!